INSIGHT
KIDS

An Imprint of Insight Editions
PO Box 3088
San Rafael, CA 94912
www.insighteditions.com

Find us on Facebook: www.facebook.com/InsightEditions
Follow us on Twitter: @insighteditions

Library of Congress Cataloging-in-Publication Data available.

ISBN: 978-1-68383-944-6

Publisher: Raoul Goff
Creative Director: Chrissy Kwasnik
Editor: Lisa Clancy
Designer: Megan Sinead Harris
Editorial Assistant: Elizabeth Ovieda
Managing Editor: Lauren LePera
Production Editor: Jennifer Bentham
Senior Production Manager: Greg Steffen

Insight Editions, in association with Roots of Peace, will plant two trees for each tree
used in the manufacturing of this book. Roots of Peace is an internationally renowned
humanitarian organization dedicated to eradicating land mines worldwide and converting
war-torn lands into productive farms and wildlife habitats. Roots of Peace will plant two
million fruit and nut trees in Afghanistan and provide farmers there with the skills and
support necessary for sustainable land use.

Manufactured in Turkey by Insight Editions

10 9 8 7 6 5 4 3 2 1

IT'S A WONDERFUL LIFE

The Illustrated Holiday Classic

ADAPTED BY PAUL RUDITIS

ILLUSTRATED BY SARAH CONRADSEN

INSIGHT
KIDS

SAN RAFAEL · LOS ANGELES · LONDON

A long time ago, back before there were televisions, before computers existed or credit cards. Long before all of that, a boy named George Bailey was growing up in a little town called Bedford Falls.

He lived in that little town never knowing that an angel named Clarence was watching over him.

(Clarence was really an Angel Second Class. That meant he hadn't earned his wings yet.)

GOWER DRUGS

GOWER DRUGS

BIJOU

THE BELLS OF ST. MARY

Clarence watched as George played with his friends.

GEORGE, HELP!

He saw the time George saved his younger brother, Harry, when he fell through the ice.

He watched as George worked at Gower's Drug Store, running deliveries and helping the customers. One day, George stopped Mr. Gower from accidentally giving the wrong medicine to a sick child.

I'LL LOVE YOU TILL THE DAY I DIE.

Mary Hatch often visited the store just to spend time with George.

Clarence watched it all.

When George got older, he worked for his father at the Bailey Brothers Building and Loan office. George's father and his Uncle Billy helped people save their money so they could buy important things, like new homes.

George didn't want to buy a new home in the little town of Bedford Falls. He dreamed of exploring the world and visiting exciting places he'd only read about in magazines.

Years later, on the night before George planned to leave Bedford Falls to travel the world, he went to a party at his old high school. There, he danced with Mary Hatch.

The dance was in the school gym, which had been built over the old pool. A jealous boy tried to ruin George and Mary's dance by opening the floor.

But that didn't stop them from dancing.

George walked Mary home
that night, wearing dry
clothes he'd found for them
in the locker room. They
made wishes by throwing
rocks at the old, abandoned
Granville house, trying to
break the windows.

George told Mary about
his dreams to see the world.

Mary didn't tell George what
she wished for, but he made
his best guess.

YOU WANT THE MOON?

JUST SAY THE WORD, AND I'LL THROW A
LASSO AROUND IT AND PULL IT DOWN.

On that same night, George's father passed away. No one trusted George's forgetful Uncle Billy to run the family business. George had to stay in Bedford Falls or else the company would close, and people would lose their money and their homes.

That was exactly what Mr. Potter wanted. He was the wealthiest man in town, and he dreamed of owning all of Bedford Falls. The Building and Loan was one of the few businesses that could stop him from taking over the entire town.

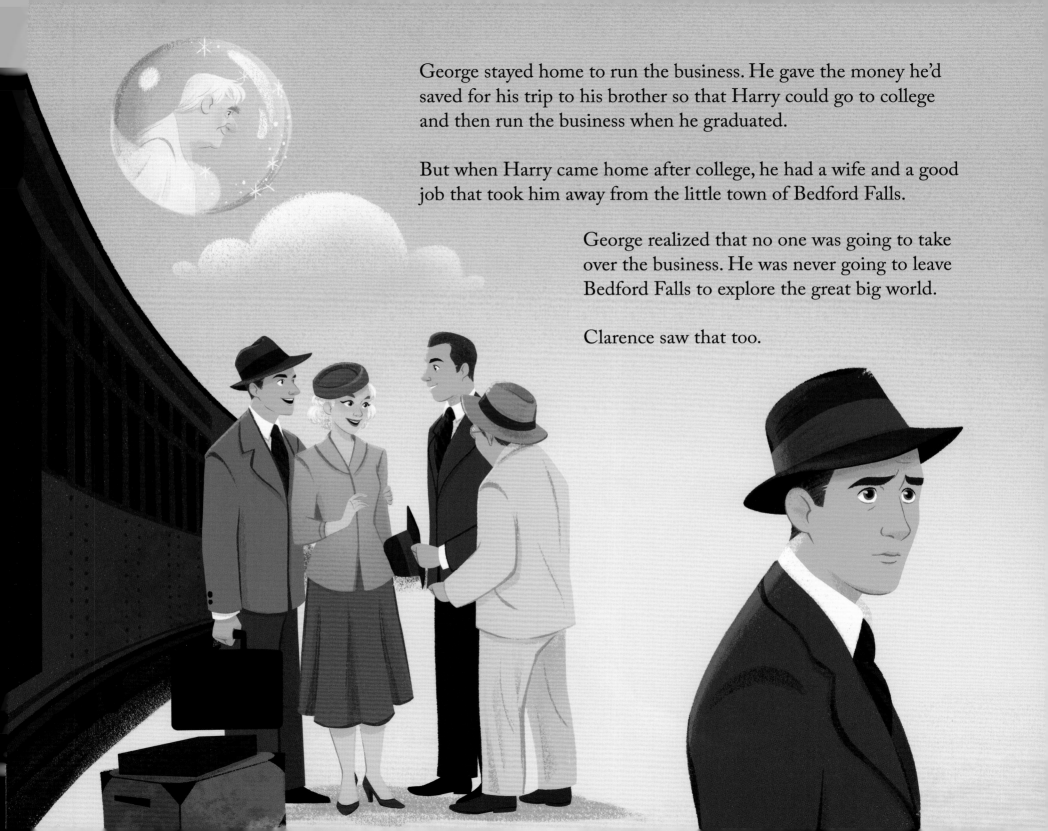

George stayed home to run the business. He gave the money he'd saved for his trip to his brother so that Harry could go to college and then run the business when he graduated.

But when Harry came home after college, he had a wife and a good job that took him away from the little town of Bedford Falls.

George realized that no one was going to take over the business. He was never going to leave Bedford Falls to explore the great big world.

Clarence saw that too.

George didn't entirely mind staying in Bedford Falls because he and Mary had fallen in love. They got engaged and planned their honeymoon. It wasn't the great big trip that George had always dreamed of, but as long as he was with Mary, it would be wonderful all the same.

On the same day as George and Mary's wedding, Mr. Potter bought the town bank and tried to take over the Building and Loan. George and Mary gave up all of their savings to help George's customers. Now, they couldn't afford to leave Bedford Falls for their honeymoon, but the company would not go out of business either.

Mr. Potter would not win.

That night, Mary told George to come to the abandoned building they'd made their wishes on. She had bought it for them with the last of their money. They would have their honeymoon in that old house in Bedford Falls.

Over the next few years, George and Mary turned that broken-down old house into a home.

They filled it with four wonderful children named Pete, Janie, Zuzu, and Tommy.

And they helped more people in Bedford Falls. For instance, George made sure that Mr. Martini got enough money to buy his own new home so he didn't have to keep renting the expensive house that Mr. Potter owned.

WELCOME TO BAILEY PARK

George helped even more people move into new homes,
and the little town of Bedford Falls began to grow.

When a war broke out overseas, George stayed in Bedford Falls, protecting people from Mr. Potter's greed and working with Uncle Billy to make sure their business stayed open.

George's brother, Harry, went off to fight in the war, where he saved hundreds of soldiers.

Everyone in town was proud of Harry. The President even gave him a special award. Uncle Billy was so excited he forgot to put the customers' money in the safe. He accidentally left it all behind when he was bragging to Mr. Potter about Harry on Christmas Eve.

It was the most important thing Uncle Billy had ever forgotten. Now, it was George's responsibility to find the money because he was the boss. If he didn't find it, he could go to jail.

George and Uncle Billy searched all over town, but they didn't find anything.

When George got home, he found his youngest daughter, Zuzu, upset because her flower had lost some petals. He couldn't fix that either, so he hid the petals in his pocket.

It was the worst Christmas ever. George was so upset that he yelled at his family, even though they'd done nothing wrong.

Mary told George to leave. Then, she started calling people for help. She could tell that her husband was very sad.

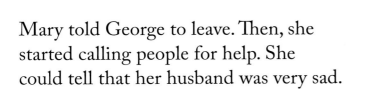

George went to the only person who could help.

Mr. Potter was the richest man in town. Surely, he could lend George the money. But the evil banker refused George's pleas for help, never admitting that he had the missing money all along.

George couldn't go home, and he couldn't go to
anyone else for help. No one in the little town of
Bedford Falls had the amount of money he needed.

George felt like a complete failure. He blamed himself for not being able to save the business, and he thought that Bedford Falls would be a better place if he weren't around to make things worse.

HELP, HELP!

That's when he heard the shouts from a man who'd fallen into the river below. George did what he always did: He dove in to help.

George saved the man and learned that it was Clarence, the Angel Second Class who had been watching over him. Clarence tried to convince George that he wasn't a failure; that his life had actually been pretty good. George didn't believe any of it, especially not the part about Clarence being an Angel Second Class.

To prove it, Clarence made George's wish come true . . .

Back at Mr. Martini's bar, Clarence tried to explain that helping George was the only way he'd earn his wings to become a full angel.

George wasn't paying attention. The place looked so different, and his friend Mr. Martini was gone. Even the bartender, Nick, was different.

EVERY TIME YOU HEAR A BELL RING, IT MEANS THAT SOME ANGEL'S JUST GOT HIS WINGS.

ding
ding

But nothing prepared George to learn what happened to his old boss from the drug store. Mr. Gower had spent years in prison because George hadn't been around to stop him from giving the wrong medicine to that sick child.

So many things were different. Was it possible that Clarence was telling the truth? Maybe George had never been born. But George still wasn't ready to believe it . . .

Not even when he discovered his daughter's flower petals were gone.

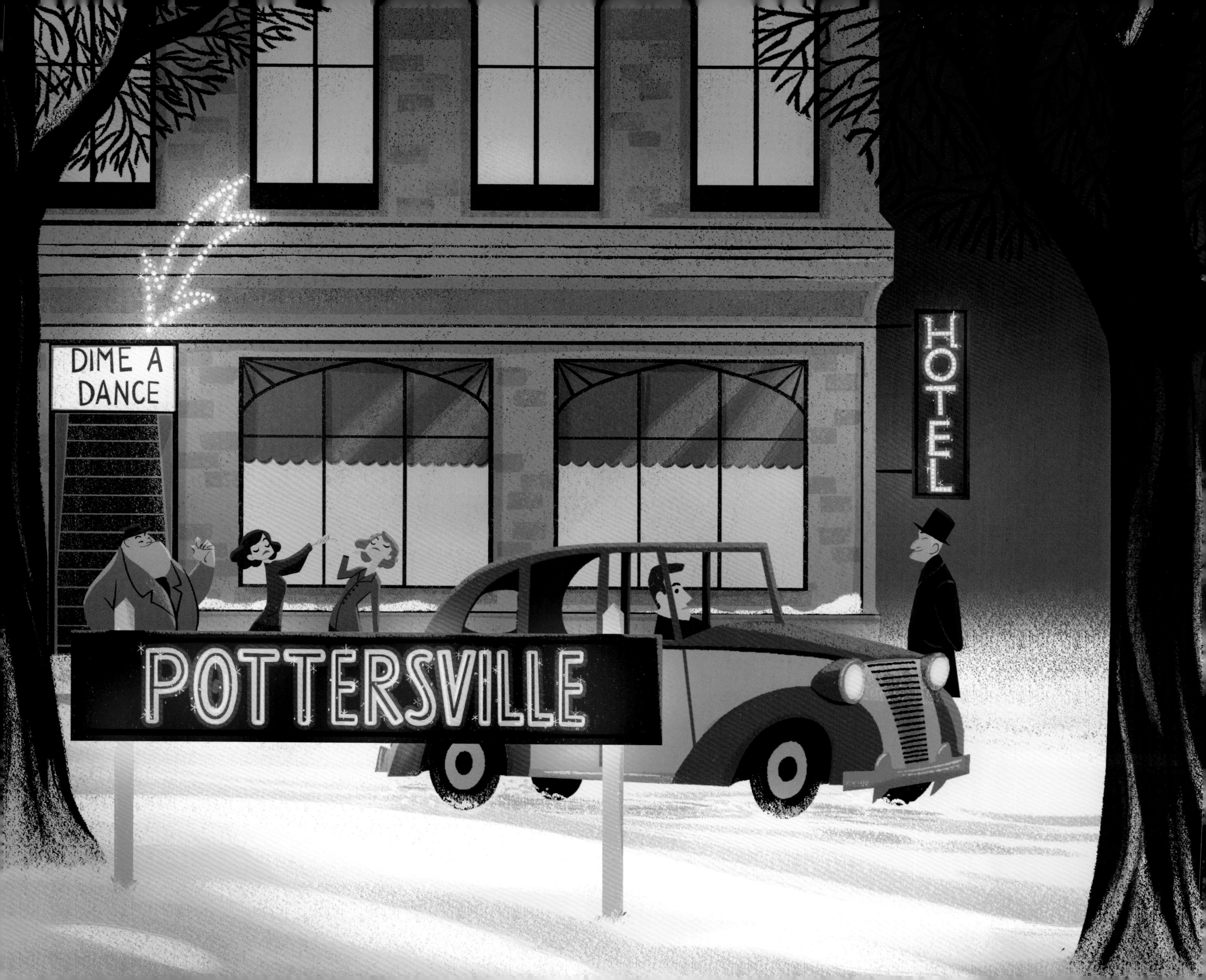
DIME A DANCE
HOTEL
POTTERSVILLE

George hurried home, surprised to find that the quiet, little town of Bedford Falls had somehow become a big, noisy town called Pottersville.

The Building and Loan had gone out of business years ago because George wasn't around to run it. With no one to stop him, Mr. Potter had taken over the entire town and made it a terrible place to live. The changes didn't end there . . .

George and Mary's home was still abandoned, as if his family had never lived there.

His own mother didn't recognize him.

YOU SEE, GEORGE, YOU REALLY HAD A WONDERFUL LIFE.

Because George had never been born, no one had been around to save his little brother when he fell through the ice. Clarence explained that, without Harry Bailey in the war, no one saved all those soldiers either.

Beloved son
HARRY BAILEY
1911 - 1919

George was horrified to discover that the love of his life, Mary Hatch, didn't recognize him. If she didn't know him, then their children had never been born either. That's why Zuzu's petals weren't in his pocket.

George was heartbroken to see that all these bad things had happened, just because he'd never been born.

George went back to the bridge where it all started, hoping that he could make everything right. He was alone again, but he called out to Clarence . . .

HELP ME, CLARENCE, PLEASE. PLEASE! I WANT TO LIVE AGAIN.

A moment after he asked for help, George's friend found him and recognized him once again. George was thrilled but not nearly as happy as when he realized that his daughter's flower petals were back in his pocket.

Everything was back to normal in Bedford Falls. Everyone on the street recognized George again. The Bailey Brothers Building and Loan was still in business. Only grumpy old Mr. Potter was upset by George's happiness.

GOWER DRUGS

GOWER DRUGS

BIJOU

THE BELLS OF ST. MARY'S

George ran all the way home. He knew the police were waiting there for him, but he didn't care. His family would be there too. And that's all that mattered.

He never expected what else would be waiting at home for him . . .

Everyone in Bedford Falls that George had ever helped turned out to support him in his time of need. They could replace all the missing money by adding together what little cash they each had. The business would survive.

George may never have left the little town of Bedford Falls, but he'd spent every day of his life helping the people around him. And those people, in turn, were there for George when he needed them.

Mr. Potter might have all the money in the bank, but money wasn't nearly as important as all the people who had come to help George in his time of need.

TEACHER SAYS EVERY TIME A BELL RINGS, AN ANGEL GETS HIS WINGS.

ding ding

On top of the money his friends had collected, George found a gift from Clarence. It seemed that George wasn't the only one whose dream had come true.

Remember George No man is a failure who has friends Thanks for the wings Clarence

Tom Sawyer

The
End